Yuck! said the Yak

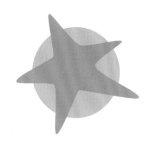

Th.

T'
a '

Maverick
Early Readers

'Yuck said the Yak'
An original concept by Alex English
© Alex English

Illustrated by Emma Levey

Published by MAVERICK ARTS PUBLISHING LTD
Studio 3A, City Business Centre, 6 Brighton Road,
Horsham, West Sussex, RH13 5BB
© Maverick Arts Publishing Limited August 2015
+44 (0)1403 256941

A CIP catalogue record for this book is available at the British Library.

ISBN 978-1-84886-176-3

www.maverickbooks.co.uk

This book is rated as: Green Band
The original picture book text for this story has been modified
by the author to be an early reader.

Yuck! said the Yak

by **Alex English**
illustrated by **Emma Levey**

A hungry yak came to stay today.

"Hello, Yak!" said Alfie.

"Would you like some toast and jam?"

"Yuck!"

said the yak.

"Have some apples," said Alfie.

"They are fresh from the tree!"

"YUCK!" said the yak.

"No apples for me!"

"Try eggs!" said Alfie.

"Or peas or cheese."

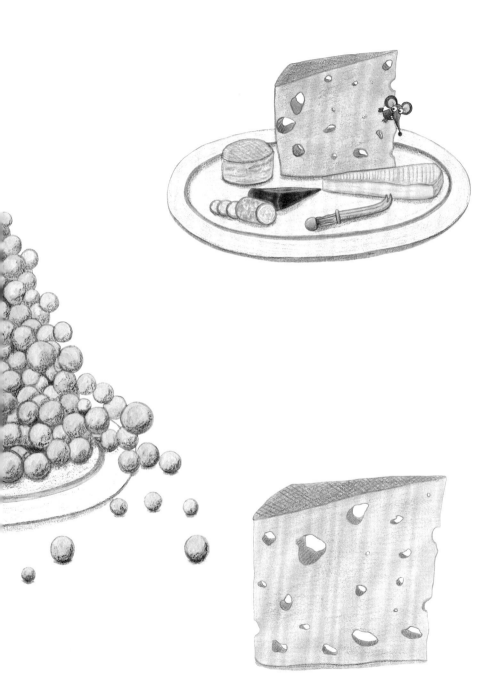

"Or strawberry jelly with

chocolate ice cream!"

But the yak said, "YUCK!"

"Hmm ..." said Alfie.

"What shall I make?"

He went in the kitchen,

and he made ...a CAKE!

"Yuck!" said the yak.

"Yuck!"

"Yuck!"

"Yuck!"

Then Alfie threw down his
plate and his cup.
"You're a VERY rude yak,"
he said. "I GIVE UP!"

"I'm a yak," said the yak.

"Yaks only like grass!"

"Grass?" said Alfie.

"How strange to like grass!"

"Yum!" said the yak.

"Would you like a small bite?"

"Yuck!" said Alfie

"Yuck!"

"Yuck!"

"Yuck!"

Quiz

1. What animal visits Alfie?
a) A bear
b) A yak
c) A dog

2. What does Alfie's guest like to eat?
a) Apples
b) Ice cream
c) Grass

3. Why does Alfie say that the yak is rude?
a) He doesn't use a knife and fork
b) He sticks his tongue out at Alfie
c) He says 'Yuck!' to everything Alfie gives him

4. But the yak said, "_____!"
a) Yuck
b) Hello
c) No

5. What does Alfie bake?
a) Cheese
b) A cake
c) Jelly

Turn over for answers

Maverick Early Readers

Our early readers have been adapted from the original picture books so that children can make the essential transition from listener to reader.

All of these books have been book banded to the industry standard and edited by a leading educational consultant.

Green

Yuck! said the Yak
by Alex English Illustrated by Emma Levey
ISBN 978-1-84886-176-3

Orange

The **Black** and White **Club**
by Alice Hemming Illustrated by Kimberley Scott
ISBN 978-1-84886-179-4

A Scarf and a Half
by Amanda Brandon Illustrated by Catalina Echeverri
ISBN 978-1-84886-177-0

Turquoise

PREPOSTEROUS RHINOCEROS
by Tracy Gunaratnam Illustrated by Marta Costa
ISBN 978-1-84886-180-0

HOCUS POCUS DIPLODOCUS
by Steve Howson Illustrated by Kate Daubney
ISBN 978-1-84886-178-7

Quiz Answers
1b, 2c, 3c, 4a.